# FU
# THE WORST WITCH

Jill Murphy started putting books together (literally with a stapler) when she was six. Her Worst Witch series, the first book of which was published in 1974, is hugely successful. She has also written and illustrated several award-winning picture books for younger children.

# FUN WITH THE WORST WITCH

## JILL MURPHY

PUFFIN

PUFFIN BOOKS

Published by the Penguin Group
Penguin Books Ltd, 80 Strand, London WC2R 0RL, England
Penguin Group (USA) Inc., 375 Hudson Street, New York, New York 10014, USA
Penguin Group (Canada), 90 Eglinton Avenue East, Suite 700, Toronto, Ontario, Canada
M4P 2Y3 (a division of Pearson Penguin Canada Inc.)
Penguin Ireland, 25 St Stephen's Green, Dublin 2, Ireland (a division of Penguin Books Ltd)
Penguin Group (Australia), 707 Collins Street, Melbourne, Victoria 3008, Australia
(a division of Pearson Australia Group Pty Ltd)
Penguin Books India Pvt Ltd, 11 Community Centre,
Panchsheel Park, New Delhi – 110 017, India
Penguin Group (NZ), 67 Apollo Drive, Rosedale, Auckland 0632,
New Zealand (a division of Pearson New Zealand Ltd)
Penguin Books (South Africa) (Pty) Ltd, Block D, Rosebank Office Park,
181 Jan Smuts Avenue, Parktown North, Gauteng 2193, South Africa

Penguin Books Ltd, Registered Offices: 80 Strand, London WC2R 0RL, England

puffinbooks.com

First published 2014
001

Text and illustrations copyright © Jill Murphy, 2014
All rights reserved

The moral right of the author and illustrator has been asserted

Set in Baskerville MT
Designed by Mandy Norman
Printed in Great Britain by Clays Ltd, St Ives plc

British Library Cataloguing in Publication Data
A CIP catalogue record for this book is available from the British Library

ISBN: 978-0-141-35256-5

www.greenpenguin.co.uk

MIX
Paper from
responsible sources
FSC
www.fsc.org    FSC™ C018179

Penguin Books is committed to a sustainable
future for our business, our readers and our
planet. This book is made from paper certified
by the Forest Stewardship Council.

This book belongs
to

# WINTER TERM

# Introduction to Miss Cackle's Academy

Miss Cackle's Academy for Witches looks more like a prison than a school, with its gloomy grey walls and turrets. Everything about it is dark and shadowy. Even the girls themselves are dressed in black gymslips, black stockings, black hob-nailed boots and grey shirts!

Turn over to meet Mildred Hubble and her friends.

# The Pupils

Fun-loving
**Enid
Nightshade**

Disaster-prone
**Mildred
Hubble**
(positively the worst
witch at Miss Cackle's
Academy)

Best friend
**Maud
Spellbody**

Snooty know-it-all
**Ethel Hallow**
(Mildred's arch-enemy)

Ethel's sidekick
**Drusilla Paddock**

# The Teachers

**Miss Cackle**
the kindly headmistress

**Miss Hardbroom**
the most terrifying form
mistress in the school

**Miss Bat**
the chanting mistress

**Miss Drill**
the gym mistress

**Miss Mould**
the art mistress

Last but not least,
Tabby
Mildred's hopeless cat

# Lost!

**Help Mildred to find her way to her dormitory before bedtime (but take care – she doesn't want to bump into Miss Hardbroom!).**

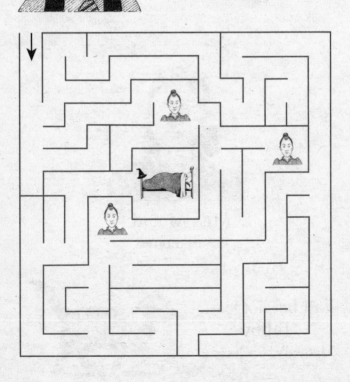

# Fancy Dress

**It's non-uniform day at Miss Cackle's Academy for Witches.**

JILL MURPHY SAYS…

'Mildred is especially fond of pink. Use your brightest crayons to colour in her unusual outfit!'

# Magic!

**Mildred can hardly believe her eyes!**
**Is this one candlestick or two faces?**
**What do you think?**

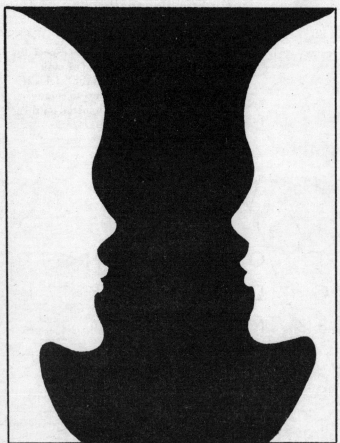

# Lost Uniform!

**Oh dear, Mildred seems to have mislaid all
of her winter uniform. She's found her tie, but
can you help her to find the rest of the items?
The words can be found in all directions,
including diagonally.**

BOOTLACES    BOOTS    CLOAK    DRESS
GYMSLIP    HAT    ROBE    SASH
SHIRT    SOCKS    STOCKINGS    TIE

| S | T | O | C | K | I | N | G | S | H |
|---|---|---|---|---|---|---|---|---|---|
| P | H | A | T | N | E | R | M | S | B |
| E | I | S | K | C | O | S | A | G | O |
| Y | B | L | H | A | R | S | R | F | O |
| T | T | O | S | W | R | O | N | E | T |
| G | R | D | R | M | T | T | K | T | L |
| R | N | N | R | I | Y | R | A | E | A |
| O | A | U | E | E | N | G | O | R | C |
| S | T | O | O | B | S | H | L | M | E |
| T | R | I | H | S | N | S | C | A | S |

# Who's who at Miss Cackle's Academy

 **Which character is tall and thin with long plaits?**

a  Maud Spellbody

b  Miss Cackle

c  Ethel Hallow

d  Mildred Hubble

 **Which character is small, has glasses and wears her hair in bunches?**

a  Enid Nightshade

b  Maud Spellbody

c  Drusilla Paddock

d  Miss Drill

 **Who is the gym mistress?**

a  Miss Drill

b  Miss Bat

c  Miss Hardbroom

d  Miss Mould

**4** **What is the name of Miss Cackle's wicked sister?**

a Angela
b Agatha
c Artemesia
d Angora

**5** **What is the name of the Chief Magician?**

a Mr Helstone
b Mr Helford
c Mr Hellimore
d Mr Hellebore

**6** **What is the name of Ethel Hallow's little sister?**

a Salamanda
b Sadie
c Sybil
d Susan

**7** **What is the name of Mildred's tortoise?**

a Cyril
b Einstein
c Archimedes
d Plato

Answers on page 78

# Mixed-up Names

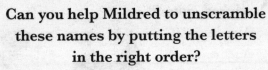

**Can you help Mildred to unscramble
these names by putting the letters
in the right order?**

INED  _ _ _ _

UDAM  _ _ _ _

HELTE  _ _ _ _ _

BAYBT  _ _ _ _ _

IDLEDMR  _ _ _ _ _ _ _

ISDULLAR  _ _ _ _ _ _ _ _

SICKCAMELS (clue: two words)

_ _ _ _  _ _ _ _ _ _

MORBIDORSMASH (clue: two words)

_ _ _ _  _ _ _ _ _ _ _ _ _

Answers on page 78

# Invisible Writing

You will need:

★ White paper

★ White wax crayon or a white candle

★ Water paint – any colour will do

★ Paint brush

★ Water

 First write your secret message on the paper using the white crayon or candle.

 To make the message appear, mix a little paint with water and brush over your paper.

And hey presto – all is revealed!

# Spot the Difference

**Everyone in the class has made a laughing potion – except for Mildred and Maud, whose spells have gone wrong!**

Can you spot **eight differences**
between these two pictures?
**Draw a circle round the changes.**

Answers on page 78

# Miss Cackle's Macaroons

**Headmistress Miss Cackle loves biscuits, especially macaroons, with her morning (and afternoon!) cup of tea. They are so delicious! Why not try making Miss Tapioca's easy recipe?**

## You will need:

★ A large mixing bowl and a wooden spoon

★ A baking tray lined with baking paper

★ 2 eggs

★ 175g ground almonds

★ 175g caster sugar

Ask a grown-up to help you, especially when using the oven.

★ Turn the oven on to Gas Mark 4, 180°C/350°F

Line a baking tray with baking paper.

 Separate the egg whites from the yolks. (Messy job!)

 Put the whites into a mixing bowl and save the yolks in a small pot in the fridge. (You won't need them for this recipe.)

 Add the ground almonds and sugar to the egg whites and fold in gently with a metal spoon until everything is mixed together.

 Roll the mixture into little balls and put them on the baking sheet (not too close together).

 Pop the tray into the oven for 12–15 minutes, or until the biscuits look golden.

 Using oven gloves, take the tray carefully out of the oven. (You may need a grown-up to help with this.)

 Cool the biscuits on a wire rack.

Eat and enjoy!

# Cracking Up!

Mildred is prone to fits of giggles which often lands her in trouble with Miss Hardbroom. Here are some of her favourite jokes:

**What do you do if a teacher rolls her eyes at you?**
*Pick them up and roll them back!*

**Why was Miss Drill cross-eyed?**
*Because she couldn't control her pupils.*

**What do cats like for breakfast?**
*Mice Crispies!*

**When is it unlucky
to see a black cat?**
*When you're a mouse!*

**What did one eye
say to the other eye?**
*Between you and me
something smells.*

**What is small and
round and giggles a lot?**
*A tickled onion!*

**Where do you
find giant snails?**
*On a giant's fingers and toes!*

# Link Words

Mildred, Maud and Enid love doing link words. Why not have a go yourself? Here's one that they've already worked out:

LEAP → **FROG** → SPAWN

★1 TABBY _ _ _ NAP

★2 SPELL _ _ _ _ WORM

★3 BACK _ _ _ _ _ FRIGHT

⭐ 4 MAGIC _ _ _ _ _ _ BOUND

⭐ 5 MOON _ _ _ _ _ SWITCH

⭐ 6 BROOM _ _ _ _ _ INSECT

⭐ 7 SPORTS _ _ _ TRIP

⭐ 8 BOTTLE _ _ _ HAT

Answers on page 79

# Chanting

**All the pupils at Miss Cackle's Academy have to learn how to chant.**

Here is the first verse of 'Eye of Toad':

Eye of toad,

Ear of bat,

Leg of frog,

Tail of cat.

Drop them in,

Stir it up,

Pour it in a silver cup.

Have a go at making up a second
verse and write it down here.

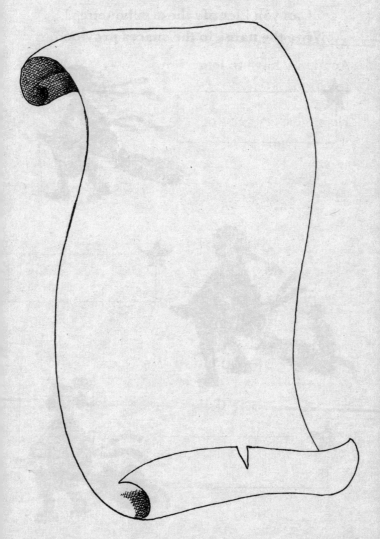

# Silhouettes

**Can you identify these silhouettes?**
**Write the name in the spaces provided.**

1.

2.

3.

**4** 

**5** 

**6** 

Answers on page 79

# Jill Murphy Says . . .

'The way I draw silhouettes is to draw an outline then fill it in with black – why don't you draw one, too?'

# Missing Links

Each of these three words
has a common word that
goes after them. Mildred
has worked out one, but is
rather stuck on the rest.
Can you help her?

FAIRY     TALL     TELL

**EXAMPLE**   **TALE**    **TALE**    **TALE**

GUIDE     HOT     PUPPY

DAY     NIGHT     BREAK

POLAR     TEDDY     KOALA

Answers on page 79

# Book of Spells

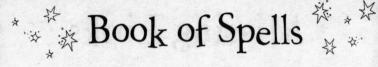

Can you find the words hidden in Mildred's *Book of Spells*? Mildred has already found FROG. Can you help her find the rest? The words can be found in all directions, including diagonally.

CAULDRON     FROG     HALLOWEEN
INGREDIENT     PONDWEED     POTION
SNAIL     SPELL     WIZARD

| P | O | N | D | W | E | E | D | I | W |
|---|---|---|---|---|---|---|---|---|---|
| L | C | E | S | O | R | F | O | N | I |
| F | A | E | T | R | O | S | V | G | Z |
| A | U | W | F | W | I | Z | A | R | D |
| N | L | O | F | K | M | P | S | E | F |
| O | D | L | L | E | P | S | N | D | R |
| I | R | L | C | G | N | F | A | I | O |
| T | O | A | A | J | R | D | I | E | S |
| O | N | H | U | O | I | B | L | N | H |
| P | W | E | G | X | T | Q | R | T | A |

Answers on page 79

# Ladders

**Starting with the word at the top of
the ladder, change one letter at a time to
get the word at the bottom of the ladder.
Use the clues to help you!**

CAT

_ _ _

_ _ _

_ _ _

_ _ _

DOG

Answers on page 79

# Secret Spell

**Know-it-all Ethel Hallow
is always boasting that she's the best
at everything. But even Ethel needs help to crack
the code for the secret shrinking spell opposite.**

| A | B | C | D | E | F |
|---|---|---|---|---|---|
| G | H | I | J | K | L |
| M | N | O | P | Q | R |
| S | T | U | V | W | X |
| Y | Z | | | | |

Using the picture clues for each letter,
mix together the ingredients below!

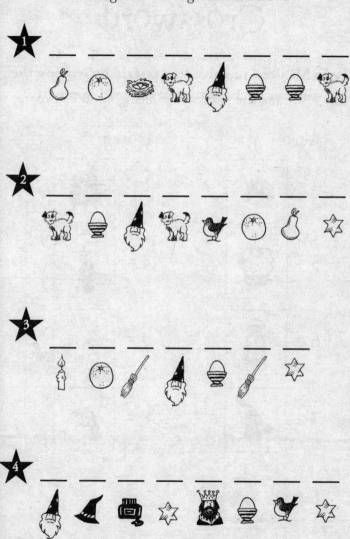

# Picture
# Crossword

Help Mildred to solve this puzzle by writing the
word for each picture in the grid opposite.

| Across | | Down | |
|---|---|---|---|
| 2 = |  | 1 = | |
| 3 = | | 4 = | |
| 6 = | | 5 = | |
| 7 = | | 8 = | 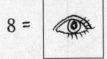 |
| 8 = | | | |

Answers on page 80

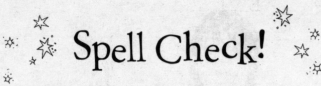

# Spell Check!

**Can you help Mildred draw a circle round the correct spelling?**

 TAIL
TALE

 SEA
SEE

 SHORE
SURE

 PAIL
PALE

**★5** EWE
YOU

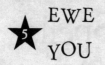

**★6** KNOT
NOT

**★7** WEATHER
WHETHER

**★8** REIN
RAIN

**★9** TOAD
TOED

**★10** PAW
POUR

# Memory Spells

Mildred needs to practise her memory skills for Miss Hardbroom's potion test.

**See how good your memory is with this memory game.**

 Get a piece of paper and write the numbers from one to ten down one side, like this:

1
2
3
4
5
6
7
8
9
10

 Now look carefully at the pictures opposite for two minutes and try to memorize them. Then close the book and write down on your piece of paper the names of all the things you can remember.

Did you remember all ten things?

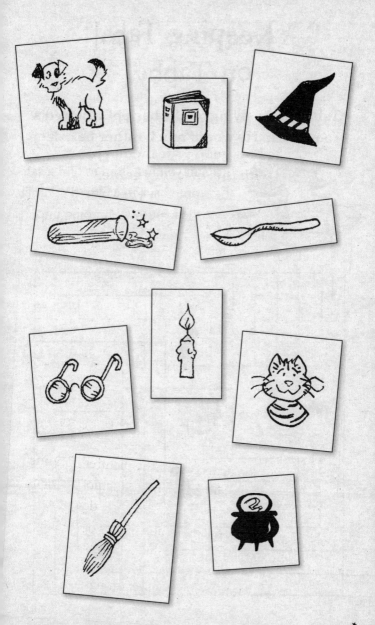

# Keeping Tabs on Tabby!

**Tabby hates flying on the back of Mildred's broomstick. He would much rather be asleep.**

Can you help him to find a safe route back to Mildred's comfy bed without bumping into any other cats?

# Frogs, Toads and Newts!

**What do you give a sick frog?**
*A hoperation.*

**Have you met Tiny?**
*He's my newt!*

**What kind of shoes do frogs like?**
*Open-toad sandals.*

**What is a frog's favourite drink?**
*Croak-a-Cola!*

# Tricky Test

**Miss Hardbroom has set a rather difficult general knowledge test. Mildred, Maud and Enid need some help.**

 **What does 'centipede' mean?**

**a** 'many legs'

**b** 'hundred-footed'

**c** 'fifty-footed'

**d** 'smelly feet'

 **What is one hundred years called?**

**a** A decade

**b** A millennium

**c** A century

**d** An era

**3** **How many legs does a spider have?**
a Four
b Twelve
c Eight
d Ten

 **4** **Which animal is the odd one out?**
a Monkey
b Dog
c Cat
d Bird

 **5** **In which month of the year does Halloween fall?**
a September
b December
c October
d March

Answers on page 80

# SUMMER
# TERM

# Design a New Swimming Costume!

Mr Rowan-Webb, the magician Mildred rescued from the school pond, has invited the whole of Mildred's form to spend an entire week at his home by the sea! The pupils are so excited, but their spirits sink when Miss Hardbroom shows them the old-fashioned swimming costumes they have to wear . . .

Mildred would be delighted if you'd design a more up-to-date swimming costume for their seaside holiday. Don't forget a swimming cap!

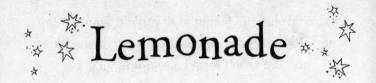

# Lemonade

It is unexpectedly hot at Grim Cove by the sea and
Mildred, Maud and Enid are feeling very thirsty.

Here is their recipe for refreshing lemonade.
**Try making some for yourself and your friends.**

### You will need:

★ 200g caster sugar

★ 250ml water

★ 250ml freshly squeezed lemon
juice (about 6 lemons)

★ 1 litre of water to dilute

Stir the sugar and 250ml of water together until the sugar has dissolved. Then stir in the lemon juice.

 Pour this into a large jug and finally add the rest of the water.

 Stir well.

 Chill in the fridge and serve with some ice cubes.

# Make a Match

**Only two of these pictures are exactly alike.**
**Which two are they?**

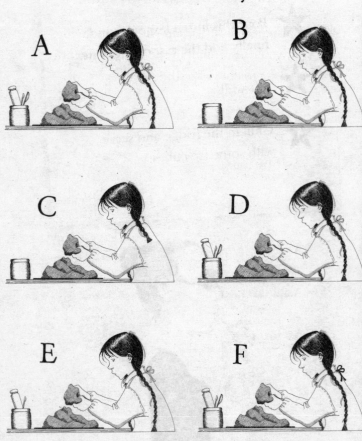

A B C D E F

Answers on page 80

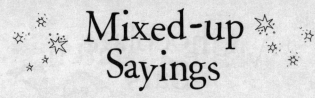

# Mixed-up Sayings

**Mildred often gets her spells mixed up,
with some disastrous results!**

She also needs some help with these sayings.
Can you draw a line to the correct picture
to complete the saying?

⭐**1** As quiet as a

⭐**2** As blind as a

⭐**3** As slow as a

⭐**4** As busy as a

⭐**5** As wise as an

⭐**6** As fat as a

⭐**7** As slippery as an

⭐**8** As cold as a

Answers on page 80

# Chocolate Bats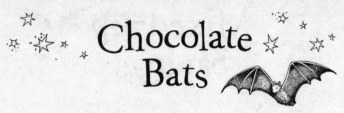

**Every night Mildred's bat friends fly home to roost in her bedroom! Now you can make your very own bat buddies!**

## You will need:

★ Chocolate mini rolls

★ Black and white fondant icing

★ Icing sugar

 Draw a bat-wing stencil on a piece of paper and cut it out.

 Roll out the black fondant icing.

 Place your stencil over the black fondant icing and with a butter knife cut out several pairs of black wings.

 Make your 'glue' using a little icing sugar and water and stick the wings around the mini rolls.

 Roll up some small balls of the white icing to make the bats eyes and complete with a smaller black ball placed in the middle.

 Use your icing sugar glue to stick the eyes on to the rolls.

You can give your bats different accessories – why not try a bow tie, a hat or even their very own broomstick!

# A Worst Witch Quiz

**How much do you know about the Worst Witch? Test your knowledge here.**

 **1** **What is the name of Mildred's school?**

**a** Miss Cackle's Academy for Wizards

**b** Miss Hardbroom's School of Sorcery

**c** Miss Drill's Training School

**d** Miss Cackle's Academy for Witches

 **2** **What does every pupil at school receive at the end of their first year?**

**a** A book of potions

**b** *How to Train Your Cat* manual

**c** A certificate

**d** *The Popular Book of Spells*

 **3** **How many terms are in a school year at Miss Cackle's Academy?**

**a** Two

**b** Three

**c** Four

**d** Five

### 4 Why is Mildred given a tabby cat, instead of a black one?

a   Because Miss Cackle had run out of black ones
b   Because tabby cats are cute
c   Because Mildred asked for one
d   Because Mildred had lost her black kitten

### 5 What is Mildred most afraid of?

a   Flying
b   Bats
c   The dark
d   Swimming

### 6 What is the picture on the school badge?

a   A tabby cat on a broomstick
b   A silver moon and a gold star
c   A black cat sitting on a yellow moon
d   A shooting star

### 7 Why does Ethel turn Mildred into a frog?

a   Because she hates Mildred
b   Because Mildred asked her to
c   She didn't mean to – it was a mistake
d   Because she wanted to get her own back for when Mildred turned her into a pig

Answers on page 80

# Summer Holiday

**Help Mildred find her way to Grim Cove for a holiday.**

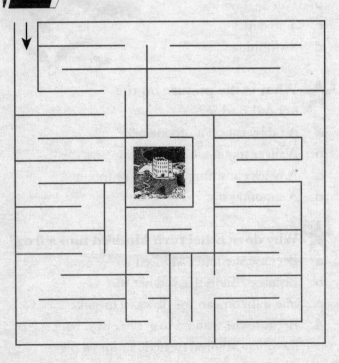

# Invisible

**Mildred and Maud have made an
invisibility potion by mistake!**

Can you fill in the rest of their bodies and
make them reappear? (Don't forget to finish
Mildred's plaits and Maud's bunches!)

# Did You Know . . . ?

 **1** A cat has about 20 muscles in each ear.

 **2** A cat uses its whiskers to check whether a space is too small for it to fit through.

 **3** Cooked mice were once used to treat whooping cough, small pox and measles. They were either roasted or fried. But if you had chicken pox, then the cure was to drink a soup made from mouse tails.

 **4** Garlic was said to cure headaches (and keep vampires away!).

 **5** A snail can sleep for three years!

**6** Bats are nocturnal which means they are active at night and spend the day sleeping. They also hang upside down when they sleep.

 **7** Even when a snake has its eyes closed, it can still see through its eyelids.

 **8** Cobwebs were once used to stop wounds bleeding. And they were used to wrap sprained wrists or ankles!

 **9** Frogs never close their eyes, even when they're sleeping!

 **10** Frogs drink through their skin!

# Number Code

**Can you work out this code to
help name the picture opposite?**

| | | | | | |
|---|---|---|---|---|---|
| A 1 | B 2 | C 3 | D 4 | E 5 | F 6 |
| G 7 | H 8 | I 9 | J 10 | K 11 | L 12 |
| M 13 | N 14 | O 15 | P 16 | Q 17 | R 18 |
| S 19 | T 20 | U 21 | V 22 | W 23 | X 24 |
| Y 25 | Z 26 | | | | |

$$\overline{\phantom{x}}_{20}\ \overline{\phantom{x}}_{8}\ \overline{\phantom{x}}_{5}$$

$$\overline{\phantom{x}}_{19}\ \overline{\phantom{x}}_{21}\ \overline{\phantom{x}}_{16}\ \overline{\phantom{x}}_{18}\ \overline{\phantom{x}}_{5}\ \overline{\phantom{x}}_{13}\ \overline{\phantom{x}}_{5}$$

,

$$\overline{\phantom{x}}_{13}\ \overline{\phantom{x}}_{1}\ \overline{\phantom{x}}_{7}\ \overline{\phantom{x}}_{9}\ \overline{\phantom{x}}_{3}\ \overline{\phantom{x}}_{9}\ \overline{\phantom{x}}_{1}\ \overline{\phantom{x}}_{14}\ \overline{\phantom{x}}_{19}$$

$$\overline{\phantom{x}}_{3}\ \overline{\phantom{x}}_{1}\ \overline{\phantom{x}}_{19}\ \overline{\phantom{x}}_{20}\ \overline{\phantom{x}}_{12}\ \overline{\phantom{x}}_{5}$$

Answers on page 80

61

# Hold On Tight!

**Have fun colouring in this picture of
Mildred as she practises her flying!**

JILL MURPHY
SAYS…

'When you colour in the
stripes on Mildred's
swimming costume,
make sure you start at
one end and finish at
the other.'

# Dot-to-Dot

**Whose stripes are these?
Starting at number 1, join the
dots to find out!**

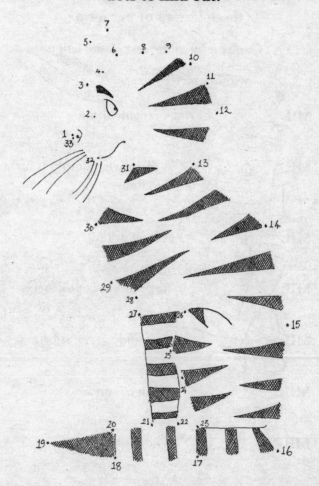

# Spell Words

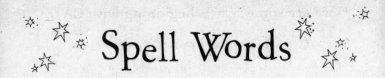

**Mildred has discovered that there are some interesting words beginning with the first three letters of her name.**

Can you fill in the rest of the letters to complete the words?

**MIL __**  A creamy drink

**MIL __**  A place where grain is turned into flour

**MIL __**  A long distance

**MIL __ __ __**  Birds like to eat this seed

**MIL __ __ __**  A mouldy green substance

**MIL __ __ __ __**  A huge number

**MIL __ __ __ __**  The Worst Witch!

# Here are some words beginning with CAT.

Can you fill in the rest of the letters
to complete the words?

**CAT** \_\_ \_\_ \_\_                 A short sleep

**CAT** \_\_ \_\_ \_\_ \_\_              Cats love the smell
of this plant

**CAT** \_\_ \_\_ \_\_ \_\_ \_\_           A tool for flinging
stones

**CAT** \_\_ \_\_ \_\_ \_\_ \_\_ \_\_ \_\_

A total disaster – a bit like Mildred!

Answers on page 80

# Summer Wordsearch

Find the words hidden in Mildred's holiday
scrapbook. Mildred has already found BEACH.
The words can be found in all directions,
including diagonally.

BEACH     BOATS     BREEZE
CLIFFS     GAMES     HOLIDAY
PEBBLES     SEAGULLS     SWIMMING
WAVES

| S | B | W | A | V | E | S | F | J | J |
|---|---|---|---|---|---|---|---|---|---|
| E | F | R | A | Q | P | Q | S | S | L |
| A | H | C | E | I | Q | E | B | W | H |
| G | R | O | Q | E | L | R | E | I | I |
| U | E | H | L | B | Z | L | A | M | G |
| L | C | X | B | I | R | E | C | M | J |
| L | R | E | V | L | D | X | H | I | K |
| S | P | O | T | Q | P | A | G | N | F |
| C | L | I | F | F | S | F | Y | G | I |
| G | A | M | E | S | B | O | A | T | S |

Answers on page 81

# Hide and Seek

Draw a straight line from one circle to another to spell something that Mildred finds at the seaside in *The Worst Witch All At Sea.*

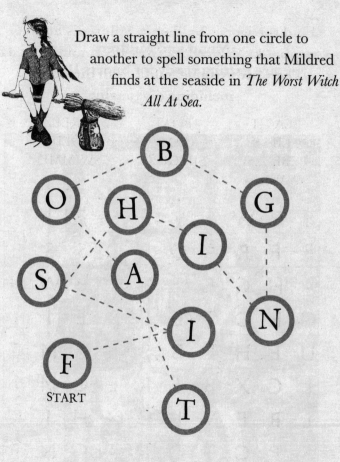

B

O   H   G

I

S   A

I   N

F

T

START

___  ___  ___  ___  ___  ___  ___

___  ___  ___  ___

# Spot the Difference

**Maud and Mildred
are getting ready for Sports Day.**

Can you spot **eight differences**
between these two pictures?
**Draw a circle round the changes.**

Answers on page 81

# ✦ ☆✦☆✦ Help! ✦ ☆✦☆

**Mildred is going to see Miss Cackle in her office but evil Miss Granite is on the prowl. Which route should Mildred take to avoid her?**

A    B          C

Answer on page 81

# Whose Birthday Is It?

**Who is the owner of this birthday cake?**
**You can find out by following the right line!**

Maud

Mildred

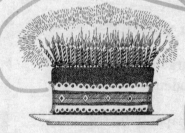

Miss Hardbroom

Ethel

Answer on page 82

# Chocolate Cornflake Crispies

Mildred has made these delicious chocolate crispies for Maud and Enid – and some extra ones for Miss Cackle!

'Oooo, don't mind if I do!'

Why not make them as a special treat for your friends!

## You will need:

★ A large mixing bowl and wooden spoon

★ 12 paper bun cases

★ A baking tray

★ 225g bar of chocolate

★ 85g of cornflakes

**1** (Ask a grown-up to help you with this bit.) Melt the chocolate by stirring it round in a large mixing bowl over a saucepan of very gently boiling water.

**2** When it is all melted and smooth, carefully take the bowl off of the saucepan.

**3** Stir in the cornflakes until they are all covered in the chocolate.

**4** Spoon the mixture into the bun cases and put them on the baking tray.

**5** Leave to cool for a bit, then pop them into the fridge until the chocolate sets hard.

# Memory Game

**Have a good look at Grid A for one minute,
then cover it up and try to put each object back
in exactly the same square on Grid B.**

GRID A

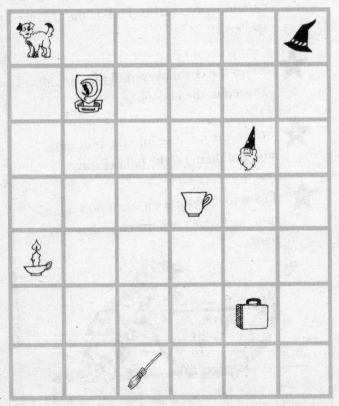

# Draw a line from each object to the square
# on Grid B where you think it belongs.

GRID B

# Spot the Difference

**Mildred has been summoned
to Miss Cackle's office again!**

Can you find **eight differences**
between these two pictures in Miss Cackle's office?
**Draw a circle round the changes.**

Answers on page 82

# Answers

## Page 11: LOST UNIFORM!

| | | | | | | | | |
|---|---|---|---|---|---|---|---|---|
| S | T | O | C | K | I | N | G | S | H |
| P | H | A | T | N | E | R | M | S | B |
| E | I | S | K | C | O | S | A | G | O |
| Y | B | L | H | A | R | S | R | F | O |
| T | T | O | S | W | R | O | N | E | T |
| G | R | D | R | M | T | T | K | T | L |
| R | N | N | R | I | Y | R | A | E | A |
| O | A | U | E | E | N | G | O | R | C |
| S | T | O | O | B | S | H | L | M | E |
| T | R | I | H | S | N | S | C | A | S |

## Pages 12–13:
## WHO'S WHO AT MISS CACKLE'S ACADEMY
1) d  2) b  3) a  4) b  5) d  6) c  7) b

## Page 14: MIXED-UP NAMES
Enid, Maud, Ethel, Tabby, Mildred, Drusilla,
Miss Cackle, Miss Hardbroom

## Page 16: SPOT THE DIFFERENCE

### Page 22: LINK WORDS
1. Cat  2. Book  3. Stage  4. Spell  5. Light  6. Stick
7. Day  8. Top

### Page 26: SILHOUETTES
1. Mildred  2. Enid  3. Maud  4. Miss Cackle
5. Ethel  6. Miss Hardbroom

### Page 29: MISSING LINKS
1. Dog  2. Time  3. Bear

### Page 30: BOOK OF SPELLS

```
P O N D W E E D I W
L C E S O R F O N I
F A E T R O S V G Z
A U W F W I Z A R D
N L O F K M P S E F
O D L L E P S N D R
I R L C G N F A I O
T O A A J R D I E S
O N H U O I B L N H
P W E G X T Q R T H
```

### Page 31: LADDERS
CAT
BAT
HAT
HOT
DOT
DOG

### Page 32: SECRET SPELL
PONDWEED  DEWDROPS  COBWEBS
WHISKERS

## Page 34: PICTURE CROSSWORD

| Across | Down |
|--------|------|
| 2 = snail | 1 = cauldron |
| 3 = owl | 2 = witch |
| 6 = lantern | 3 = flame |
| 7 = hat | 8 = eye |
| 8 = Ethel | |

## Page 36: SPELL CHECK

1. Tail  2. Sea  3. Shore  4. Pail  5. Ewe  6. Knot
7. Weather  8. Rain  9. Toad  10. Paw

## Page 42: TRICKY TEST

1) b  2) c  3) c  4) d – the others are mammals  5) c

## Page 50: MAKE A MATCH

A and D

## Page 51: MIXED-UP SAYINGS

1. Mouse  2. Bat  3. Snail  4. Bee  5. Owl  6. Pig
7. Eel  8. Fish

## Page 54: A WORST WITCH QUIZ

1) a  2) d  3) a  4) a  5) c  6) c  7) d

## Page 60: NUMBER CODE

The Supreme Magician's Castle

## Pages 64–65: SPELL WORDS

MILK  MILL  MILE  MILLET
MILDEW  MILLION  MILDRED

CATNAP  CATMINT
CATAPULT  CATASTROPHE

## Page 66: SUMMER WORDSEARCH

| | | | | | | | | | |
|---|---|---|---|---|---|---|---|---|---|
| S | B | W | A | V | E | S | F | J | J |
| E | F | R | A | Q | P | Q | S | S | L |
| A | H | C | E | I | Q | E | B | W | H |
| G | R | O | Q | E | L | R | E | I | I |
| U | E | H | L | B | Z | L | A | M | G |
| L | C | X | B | I | R | E | C | M | J |
| L | R | E | V | L | D | X | H | I | K |
| S | P | O | T | Q | P | A | G | N | F |
| C | L | I | F | F | S | F | Y | G | I |
| G | A | M | E | S | B | O | A | T | S |

## Page 67: HIDE AND SEEK

Fishing boat

## Page 68: SPOT THE DIFFERENCE

## Page 70: HELP!

Route B

## Page 71: WHOSE BIRTHDAY IS IT?

Miss Hardbroom

## Page 76: SPOT THE DIFFERENCE

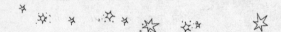

Get to know Mildred Hubble
from her very first disastrous day!

*She may be the worst witch at Miss Cackle's Academy
for Witches, but she's the best friend you could ever have.*

puffin.co.uk

Winter Term starts surprisingly well for
Mildred Hubble. But when she sees a wishing star
things quickly take an unexpected turn.
Can she put things right or does this latest
disaster spell the end for the Worst Witch?

'Millions of young readers have fallen under the
spell of Jill Murphy's Worst Witch' – *Sunday Express*

puffin.co.uk

# Bright and shiny and sizzling with fun stuff . . .

# puffin.co.uk

## WEB FUN

**UNIQUE and exclusive digital content!**
Podcasts, photos, Q&A, Day in the Life of, interviews
and much more, from Eoin Colfer, Cathy Cassidy,
Allan Ahlberg and Meg Rosoff to Lynley Dodd!

## WEB NEWS

The **Puffin Blog** is packed with posts and photos from
Puffin HQ and special guest bloggers. You can also sign up
to our monthly newsletter **Puffin Beak Speak**

## WEB CHAT

**Discover something new** EVERY month –
books, competitions and treats galore

## WEBBED FEET

(Puffins have funny little feet and
brightly coloured beaks)

# Point your mouse our way today!

# It all started with a Scarecrow

**Puffin is over seventy years old.**
Sounds ancient, doesn't it? But Puffin has never been
so lively. We're always on the lookout for the next big
idea, which is how it began all those years ago.

Penguin Books was a big idea from the mind of
a man called Allen Lane, who in 1935 invented
the quality paperback and changed the world.
**And from great Penguins, great Puffins grew,
changing the face of children's books forever.**

The first four Puffin Picture Books were hatched in 1940 and the
first Puffin story book featured a man with broomstick arms called
Worzel Gummidge. In 1967 Kaye Webb, Puffin Editor, started the
Puffin Club, promising to **'make children into readers'**.
She kept that promise and over 200,000 children became devoted
Puffineers through their quarterly instalments of *Puffin Post*.

Many years from now, we hope you'll look back and
remember Puffin with a smile. **No matter what your age
or what you're into, there's a Puffin for everyone.**
The possibilities are endless, but one thing is for sure:
whether it's a picture book or a paperback, a sticker book
or a hardback, **if it's got that little Puffin
on it – it's bound to be good.**

# WORLD BOOK DAY *fest*

## Want to **READ** more?

 **Visit** your LOCAL BOOKSHOP

- Get some great recommendations for what to read next

- Meet your favourite authors & illustrators at brilliant events

- Discover books you never even knew existed!

 **FIND YOUR LOCAL BOOKSHOP** WWW.BOOKSELLERS.ORG.UK/BOOKSHOPSEARCH

 **Join** your LOCAL LIBRARY

You can browse and borrow from a HUGE selection of books and get recommendations of what to read next from expert librarians—all for FREE! You can also discover libraries' wonderful children's and family reading activities.

 **FIND YOUR LOCAL LIBRARY** WWW.FINDALIBRARY.CO.UK

 **GET ONLINE!** Visit **WWW.WORLDBOOKDAY.COM** to discover a whole *new* world of books!

- Downloads and activities
- Cool games, trailers and videos
- Author events in your area
- News, competitions and new books —all in a **FREE** monthly email

 **AND MORE!**